PUFFIN BOOKS
BLACK BEAUTY

'Wonderful!' the Squire exclaimed, turning to John and me. 'John, what do you think about Black Beauty? We'll call him Black Beauty!'

John smiled widely. 'That's a lovely name!'

I thought so, too. Black Beauty! What a splendid, magnificent, fantastic name!

I decided then and there that my name would *always* be Black Beauty. No matter what.

BLACK BEAUTY

Based on the screenplay by
Caroline Thompson

From the classic novel by
Anna Sewell

Adapted by
Catherine R. Daly

PUFFIN BOOKS

PUFFIN BOOKS

Published by the Penguin Group
Penguin Books Ltd, 27 Wrights Lane, London W8 5TZ, England
Penguin Books USA Inc., 375 Hudson Street, New York, New York 10014, USA
Penguin Books Australia Ltd, Ringwood, Victoria, Australia
Penguin Books Canada Ltd, 10 Alcorn Avenue, Toronto, Ontario, Canada M4V 3B2
Penguin Books (NZ) Ltd, 182–190 Wairau Road, Auckland 10, New Zealand

Penguin Books Ltd, Registered Offices: Harmondsworth, Middlesex, England

First published by in the USA by Western Publishing, Inc. 1994
Published in Puffin Books 1995
1 3 5 7 9 10 8 6 4 2

Filmset in 13/16 Monophoto Baskerville

Printed in England by Clays Ltd, St Ives plc

Contents

1

My Early Home

From the start I depended on humans. This is a story about trusting them, losing trust in them, and finally getting it back again.

I was born late one night in the year 1880 on an estate owned by my mother's master, a good, kind man named Farmer Grey. My mother, Duchess, used to tell me how she anxiously watched as I, a small spindly-legged coal-black foal with a white star in the middle of my forehead and one white foot, struggled with all my might to stand up on my own. Finally, she said, Farmer Grey had to help me to my feet for my first drink of mother's milk.

My mother and I spent most of our time in a

beautiful large green meadow in the countryside. There was a pond of clear water to drink from, with tall shady trees on one side and cat's-tails and water lilies on the deep end. We could see Farmer Grey's house from one side of the field and a running brook with a steep bank from the other. It was a lovely place.

At first I stayed as close to my mother as I could. But as I grew, my curiosity got the better of me and I learned the joys of running, jumping and playing. It was a peaceful and comfortable life, with hardly a care in the world. That is, until one unforgettable day in the early spring when I was almost two years old.

It was the day of a foxhunt. Excitement buzzed in the air as the sound of barking dogs and blasting horns reached the meadow. A flock of crows burst out of a nearby tree, and rabbits and other small animals ran away, frightened by the noise. The pack of hounds had found their prey and were headed in our direction, closely followed by a group of huntsmen in scarlet coats perched on the backs of huge horses. My mother and I trotted over to a corner of the field to watch the hunt pass by.

When the dogs approached the wide brook,

they easily clambered over the steep bank. However, horse after horse attempted the jump but could not make it. Then we saw one rider who sat astride a large black horse approach the bank. He whipped his mount mercilessly and forced him to take the jump.

My mother held her breath and I watched in horror as horse and rider both somersaulted in the air, plummeting into the brook. There was a stunned silence among the other riders as the great horse struggled to the bank and collapsed. The hapless rider clutched his shattered leg and wailed in pain.

Although the men tugged and pulled, the mighty beast would not, could not, rise.

Farmer Grey rushed across the meadow. He climbed over the fence and surveyed the scene, shaking his head sadly. The fallen horse looked at our master, wild-eyed with terror.

'Rob Roy . . . Not you . . .' Farmer Grey said quietly.

There was no denying the truth. The beautiful horse's leg was broken. There was nothing anyone could do to save him.

'Does anybody have a pistol?' one of the huntsmen shouted.

Farmer Grey silently raised his arm, revealing the gun he had clutched in his hand.

'I do,' he said, his voice thick with emotion.

The few moments Farmer Grey took to aim the gun seemed to take for ever. My mother and I jumped at the sound of the gunshot. Then we stared in silence at the terrible sight of the black horse lying broken and still at the brook's edge.

Both horse and rider had broken their legs. The man's leg could be fixed, but the horse's could not. Later my mother told me she had known Rob Roy. He was a good bold horse . . . and now he was dead. All for the sake of sport.

My mother never went to that corner of the field again.

The next year, when I was three, Farmer Grey took me into the training ring. He had the head groom walk me, turn me and trot me in front of him. The whole time Farmer Grey kept singing to me softly, 'There's a clever boy . . . There's a clever boy . . . There's a clever little fellow.' His quiet tone soothed me, although I still had no idea why my master was studying me so carefully. Then he turned to the head groom and said, 'I won't be selling him till he's a good strong four-year-old. Colts shouldn't have to work like horses till they're grown up.'

He sent me to spend the next year in the big pasture with the other colts.

I had a fine year, spending my days galloping with the colts. We had great fun racing each other, kicking our legs and nipping each other. But by the time the year was up and I had turned four, I was quite nearly full grown.

It was time for Farmer Grey to keep the promise he made the year before. It was time for me to be broken in.

One day I was playing with the other foals when suddenly there was an ear-piercing whistle. We all stopped in our tracks and whipped round to find the source of the sound. It was the head groom. He bent over to pick up the halter and lead he'd set down by the fence and opened the gate. Then he stepped into the pasture, heading straight for me.

'It's time for school, Blackie,' he said, fitting the halter over my head and leading me away from my friends. I watched as my companions scampered away, relieved that it was not yet their turn. I sighed and followed the head groom. He laughed out loud and said, 'It'll be OK, young fellow. Lucky for you, too – the master wants to break you in himself and he's the gentlest horseman in the county.' He patted my neck gently as we made our way to the training ring.

Breaking in a horse is not as simple as it may sound. It involves teaching a horse to wear a saddle and bridle and carry a passenger on his back. The horse must be obedient and move neither too fast nor too slow, and go exactly the way the rider wishes to go. The horse must also learn to wear a collar, crupper and blinkers and to stand silent and still as they are put on. The horse must allow a cart or wagon to be attached to him and must always, always listen to his master and go as fast or slow as the master wishes, even though the horse may be tired or hungry. The horse must always be calm and never speak to another horse, bite or kick. The worst part is that he may neither jump for joy nor lie down if he is tired, once the harness is on. Breaking in is a very serious business.

But Farmer Grey had a soft, gentle touch and a kind voice – not to mention an ample supply of grain – which made my training as painless and as pleasant as it could possibly be.

Still, it did take a while for me to get used to the snaffle bit – Farmer Grey would feed me grain from his hand, then slip the shining steel bit into my mouth. The first time, I tried to spit the nasty cold metal out of my mouth, but Farmer Grey was slow and patient and there it stayed. If you've never had a bit in your mouth, you can't know how bad it feels. Cold hard steel between your teeth and over your tongue – it's terrible!

After the bit was in, the bridle's head-piece was fitted over my ears and the throat latch was fastened. The saddle was next. It spooked me at first, but it was not as bad as I had anticipated.

The next thing I knew, it was time to get a set of iron shoes. I watched in astonishment as the blacksmith pulled a red-hot horseshoe out of a blazing fire, set it on the bottom of my hoof, dropped it into cold water, then proceeded to nail it to my hoof. What a curious thing!

When Farmer Grey took me for a ride for the first time, I took it slowly at first. I wasn't used to having a grown man sitting on my back. But when I got accustomed to the weight of the rider, the iron shoes that made my feet feel stiff and heavy, the pull of hands on the reins, the sawing of the bit in my mouth, and the heels in my sides, I realized I felt rather proud to be carrying my master.

This riding business turned out to be . . . perfectly glorious!

Our first ride was something I will never forget. I felt as if I could have ridden all day and it seemed as if we did! I saw trees, streams, forests – more than I had ever seen before in my sheltered life in the meadow. We even saw a miniature-horse farm! I felt as big as a Clydesdale as I passed through a herd of tiny horses that barely reached my knees.

At first I was spooked by anything unusual: for instance, when we turned a corner and suddenly came upon a huge draft horse pulling a cart, and then another time when a rabbit darted in front of me across the road. But I soon got used to these distractions – until we rode by the railway tracks.

That was when I witnessed the most frightening thing I'd ever seen in my life: a train – a huge, loud, thundering, smoke-belching railway train. Farmer Grey tried his best to calm me down, but I couldn't help but tremble at the terrible noise it made. Farmer Grey said I'd get used to the 'blasted things' one day, and believe it or not, I actually did.

There are many horses who are terrified at the sight or sound of a train, but thanks to my master's foresight in getting me used to them, I am now as fearless at a train station as I was in that sweet meadow of my youth.

There were so many things about horses that my kind master knew. As we neared home and entered a narrow, rocky lane, he slowed me down to keep me from picking up a stone. Despite his precautions, a stone did indeed get wedged into my hoof. He carefully removed it. 'They are wicked things,' he told me. 'You could get a nasty bruise, or worse.'

I had no idea – I still had a lot to learn!

When I returned to the stable after my amazing first ride, my mother was being groomed in her stall, impatiently waiting for our return. She nickered in greeting as we arrived.

'How was he, Mr Grey?' the head groom asked, pausing a moment from brushing my mother's rich brown coat.

Farmer Grey dismounted and gave me the highest compliment I could ever receive. 'As pleasant and bold and sure . . . as his mother,' he said, smiling at the two of us.

I whinnied loudly in reply.

Soon afterwards I was introduced to the double harness. My mother was my partner. The collar was heavy, and the blinkers went on both sides of my eyes, so I could only see straight ahead. My tail was doubled over and poked through the crupper – an awful stiff strap that went right under my tail. It was terribly uncomfortable.

My mother offered me some advice. She said I should always do my work with a good will, lift up my feet in a trot and never, never bite or kick. This, I must admit, was sometimes hard to follow. But tempting though it may have been to disobey, I listened to my mother. And in time, I grew to pull the carriage as well as she, or nearly as well.

All too soon it was time for me to go to my new home, wherever that might be. My mother was sure our master would only sell me to good people, though a horse never knows who will buy him . . . it's all chance for us.

When we said good-bye, my mother and I nuzzled together one last time.

She urged me to do my best . . . and I always have. I've tried to make her proud and to keep up my good name.

I went to live in Birtwick Park with Squire Gordon and his family.

I never saw my mother again.

2

Birtwick Park

I got my first glimpse of my new home as John Manly, the head groom, rode me up to the front gates of Birtwick Park. And what a lovely place it was. I could see several gardens and the large manor house, where Squire and Mistress Gordon lived with their three children. Behind these lay the home paddock, a large orchard and the stables.

Mr Manly had a kind, pleasant voice and gentle ways. It was evident that Farmer Grey had chosen well for me.

As soon as we approached the house, my new master and his wife came out and stood on the porch. Squire Gordon had a pleasant face and seemed quite attentive to his lovely but frail-looking wife, who was wrapped in a warm shawl. I could hear him trying to convince her to go back inside.

'Please stay inside, my dear,' he said. 'You're still much too weak.'

'I won't break,' his wife replied. 'I want to see him.'

'He's a horse,' the Squire said. 'No more, no less. I promise.

'See,' he said, pointing to me as we came to a stop by the front steps. 'A horse.'

'What a beautiful horse!' Mistress Gordon said as she smiled widely, her eyes shining.

'Beauty is as beauty does,' the Squire replied. Then he turned to his groom. 'How was he, John?'

'Perfect, sir. They were shooting rabbits near Highwood and the guns went off – he pulled up a touch and looked but didn't step off the track,' he replied. 'Did you, young fellow?' he asked, patting me.

Throughout John's explanation, Mistress Gordon had been looking at me carefully. 'What shall we call him?' she asked her husband.

'We'll decide over tea,' he replied, looking at

her worriedly. 'You really must get out of the cold air.'

But the mistress continued studying me. 'He's as black as ebony,' she said to herself. 'Ebony, E-bony,' she tested the name, wrinkling her nose. 'No – it sounds like bones.' That seemed to make her sad.

'Settle him in the stables, will you, John?' Squire Gordon asked gently.

'Pleasure, sir,' John replied and turned to lead me away. Out of the corner of my eye I could see the mistress still watching me.

Squire Gordon took her arm protectively. 'Let's make it simple,' he said. 'Let's call him Blackbird . . . after your uncle's old horse.'

Mistress Gordon shook her head. 'Blackbird was ugly. *And* mean-tempered.'

Suddenly a smile crossed her face. 'Wait! You've already named him!'

'Pardon?' her confused husband asked.

'Beauty is as beauty does!' she replied.

'But, darling, that's not a name.'

'Yes, it is! Beauty! Black Beauty!' she said happily.

'Wonderful!' the Squire exclaimed, turning to John and me. 'John, what do you think about

Black Beauty? We'll call him Black Beauty!'

John smiled widely. 'That's a lovely name!'

I thought so, too. Black Beauty! What a splendid, magnificent, fantastic name!

I decided then and there that my name would *always* be Black Beauty. No matter what.

In one day I had a new master, a new home, a new name and a stableful of new horses to meet.

The stable had roomy stalls and swinging windows that looked out on the yard and let in sun and air. It looked as if it would be a comfortable and pleasant place to live. As John led me to my box stall, I had to pass by the other horses who were already in their stalls. I'll never forget how frightening it was. As I was the new horse in the stable, one by one they gave me a bit of an initiation. One horse snorted loudly at me as I passed, another tried to nip me, yet another bared his teeth. But the worst was when a tall chestnut mare squealed shrilly and lunged, nearly knocking me over.

'Steady there, Ginger! Show some manners!' John Manly scolded.

I was disappointed to realize that I was to

live in the stall next door to this nervous horse. Whenever I turned to look at Ginger, she would pin her ears back and bare her teeth at me.

John explained her behaviour by telling me, 'She's only just arrived herself. She'll come round.'

I wasn't so sure about that. I guessed that time would tell.

The next person I met was Joe Green, John Manly's nephew. It was his first day at Birtwick Manor, too, and he was obviously quite nervous around horses.

After John quickly removed my saddle and bridle and brushed me, he turned to Joe and said, 'Give me a hand with Black Beauty here.'

'Who?' asked the boy nervously. 'There's *another* one?'

'You put on the headcollar while I get some water,' John insisted.

'On my first day?' Joe gulped.

John shook his head. 'If you don't start on your first day, when do you plan on starting?' He pointed to the collar, then to me. 'Head-collar. Horse's head. You can work it out.'

John left to get me some water while Joe

struggled along – he tried the headcollar sideways and upside down and ended up fitting the nosepiece over my ears. It was not very comfortable.

John returned with the water and proceeded to fill my bucket. 'For horses, Joe, you don't want to draw water that's too cold. It'll give 'em a terrible bellyache.' He turned around. 'How are you getting along with that headcollar?'

Joe stepped aside and pointed proudly at me. John looked at his nephew's handiwork, trying to hold back a smile.

'That's an interesting idea, but it goes like this,' he said, showing his embarrassed nephew the proper positioning.

'Oh,' said Joe, looking sheepish.

'Now for his rug,' said John.

'Rug?' echoed the confused boy, looking down at the floor.

'No, not that kind of rug.' The head groom laughed as he threw a horse blanket over my back and buckled it on.

He turned to his nephew. 'Off with the headcollar, Joe.'

'We just put it on!' protested the boy.

'So you could learn,' John explained with a smile.

Joe sighed and removed the headcollar.

'Learning makes me very hungry,' he said when he had finally finished.

'Shall we get you something to eat before you take the headcollars off and put the blankets on the rest of the horses?' John asked.

'Yes, please!' begged the boy.

Poor Joe – there were so many new things for him to learn!

In addition to the unfriendly Ginger, I also met Merrylegs, the adored pet of the Gordons' young daughters, Jessica and Molly. The little grey pony loved the little girls almost as much as he disliked their teasing older brother, Alfred.

Shortly after Joe and John left for their supper, I saw Merrylegs for the first time. I heard a commotion from beyond the stableyard and looked out of the door. I saw two pretty little girls on the back of a handsome dapple-grey pony. The girls screamed as a bigger boy chased them, brandishing a big stick.

'Don't touch him, Alfred! Get away! He's tired!' Jessica yelled.

'Get away! He's tired!' Molly, the smaller of the two, echoed.

'Lazy pony, I'll make him run!' Alfred shouted as he grabbed at the reins.

'Merrylegs hates you!' the two girls yelled at him. But that meant nothing to the determined boy. He grabbed the reins, pushed the girls off the horse's back, and hopped on, digging in his heels and whacking the pony with the stick. 'Charge!' he yelled.

But instead of running, the stubborn little pony lay down. The boy got up and tugged at the reins furiously, shouting, 'Get up, get up, you stupid thing!'

All of a sudden Merrylegs stood up, and the seemingly victorious boy climbed on. Then, in a flash, the horse sat down and Alfred slid unceremoniously off his back. The girls giggled delightedly as Merrylegs scrambled up and dashed for the stables.

Moments later, the pony ran in and mischievously opened several of the horses' stalls. The newly freed horses ran out into the yard.

Then the little pony darted to his own stall, which happened to be on the other side of mine, and let himself in.

I looked at the little energetic fellow next to me. Merrylegs was certainly the perfect name for him. The Gordons seemed to have a way with naming their horses!

Alfred was close behind, followed by his little sisters. He was furious. But as soon as he stepped inside the pony's stall, Merrylegs expertly slipped past him. The girls parted to let their pet escape. John and Joe returned to the stable-yard just in time and almost collided with the little pony. Joe looked panic-stricken and tried to run away. His uncle grabbed him by the arm and held him back.

Meanwhile Alfred strode after the little fellow, the stick still held in his hand. But John knew just how to handle the situation.

Stepping into the boy's path, John stopped him, saying, 'Better to let Joe catch them, Master Alfred. He needs the practice.' He turned to Joe. 'Go on now and round them up.'

Joe hesitated for a second, then smiled confidently. 'Right. No problem,' he said and headed off, intent on making the horses obey.

But the horses ignored the small boy's attempts to round them up. Merrylegs had a grand time evading the boy, running around and stirring up the other horses.

John turned to the still-angry Alfred. 'Thank you for offering help, Master Alfred. I expect it's time for your supper, isn't it?'

There was nothing else for the embarrassed boy to do. 'Yes. I expect it is,' he replied, dejected that his plan had failed.

As Alfred left, followed by his two sisters, John brought the seemingly out-of-control situation to order by grabbing a bucketful of oats and shaking it noisily. 'Come along, everybody,' he shouted.

The horses clustered around John and the bucket. It was funny to see little Joe, in shock at how easily his uncle took care of the problem. I suddenly realized how much I liked this place already. I was so happy and pleased with my new surroundings that I impulsively started wagging my head back and forth with my lip curled back, a big smile on my face.

Joe was frightened. 'What's he doing?' he asked John anxiously.

'He wants to play, too,' his uncle replied, laughing.

'No, I've had enough playing for today!' the young boy stated.

John laughed again. This made me smile and wag my head even more. I knew I was going to enjoy living in Birtwick Park.

I hoped I'd live there for ever.

3

Making Friends

Merrylegs and I fast became friends, but it took longer to get to know Ginger. The little pony and I wondered if she would ever calm down.

The first time that Merrylegs, Ginger and I were turned out together in the orchard, we instinctively rushed towards each other. But as soon as we got close to Ginger, she stopped and squealed shrilly, warning us to stay away. I obeyed her command, but plucky little Merrylegs did not. The little pony pawed the grass and held his ground. The two horses wheeled around, snorting at each other.

Ginger looked awfully angry – her ears were pinned back and we could see the whites of her eyes. She chased us all around the orchard. But to our surprise and pleasure, pretty soon we were chasing *her*.

Then Ginger and I would chase Merrylegs, and Merrylegs and Ginger would chase me. We ran through the orchard, galloping up and down the hill and in between the trees.

Our progress was slow but sure. Over time, the acquaintance we made deepened into true affection.

Those horses were two of the dearest friends I would ever know.

Soon afterwards it was decided that I would be hitched to the Squire's carriage. It was my first time in double harness with a horse other than my mother. And just my luck, my partner was the high-strung Ginger. Grazing beside a horse is one thing, but pulling a carriage with her was another thing altogether. She shook her head and pawed the ground nervously as John finished harnessing her to the carriage.

'What's the matter with her?' Joe asked.

'Her old owners must have battered her about,' John replied. 'Let this be a lesson to you. Good people make good horses, Joe. Bad people make bad ones. If we treat her well and give her her head, she'll come around soon enough.'

As Joe backed me towards my side of the carriage pole, Ginger pinned back her ears and bared her teeth at me.

I thought of how lucky I had been with my masters. So far they had only been good people. I felt sorry for Ginger, because now I realized why she behaved the way she did.

But I was still apprehensive. I hoped that this arrangement would work out.

Surprisingly, working with Ginger was much better than I had expected. My mother had taught me to work hard and do an honest day's work. For all her mistreatment, Ginger also was a good, hard worker. I admired her for it. And, best of all, our paces matched perfectly, much to the delight of John and our new master.

My favourite times were when Ginger, Merrylegs and I would graze together under the gnarled old trees in the apple orchard, playing and chasing each other through the trees on the hill.

Sometimes Ginger and Merrylegs would perform a dance for me, sidestepping together, then simultaneously standing on their back feet and spinning around.

Those were the happy days . . . the happiest days of my life.

But a horse's life isn't all play. There's work to be done, too. One rainy day I was chosen to take Squire Gordon to town. I was hitched to a light, high-wheeled dog-cart, which I enjoyed pulling, and we set off.

John and I waited patiently outside the office building where Squire Gordon was conducting business with his lawyer. It began to rain harder. Finally the Squire and his lawyer stepped out of the building. John hopped down and removed the tarpaulin he'd put on my back to protect me from the rain.

The lawyer approached and looked at me with an appraising eye. 'Lovely animal,' he said, turning to Squire Gordon. 'It's a pity you don't have him more fashionably fitted out.'

'Good grief!' the Squire exploded. 'If we could act *more* according to common sense and *less* according to fashion —'

Just then the lawyer's carriage, pulled by a handsome pair of greys, appeared around the corner. They were harnessed up with bearing reins, which were so tightly buckled that they forced the horses to stand with their heads held unnaturally high and their necks arched. It looked extremely uncomfortable.

'You can't deny that my horses look the picture of elegance,' the lawyer said proudly.

'You mean the picture of cruelty!' the Squire spat out. 'Can they breathe properly with their heads held so high?' he asked as he pulled his own head back, demonstrating how hard it was to breathe in that position.

'But I like to see my horses' heads up!' the solicitor retorted.

This further angered Squire Gordon. 'So that they can't throw their weight forward when they need to? So that they put too much pressure on their joints? Count your lucky stars my wife isn't here. She'd give you such an earful –'

'It seems to me I'm getting an earful *now*,' the lawyer interrupted.

Squire Gordon stared at the man, then said, 'I might do better to take my business elsewhere.'

'You'd take away your business over the way I treat my horses?' the solicitor asked in disbelief.

Squire Gordon stared at him in stony silence, and the bewildered lawyer looked at John, as if for help. John nodded his head, answering the question.

'Right,' the solicitor said as he loosened the reins on the greys.

'Thank you,' Squire Gordon said. He climbed up beside John and took my reins.

When the lawyer thought he was alone again, he tightened the reins on the greys once again. But when he looked up, he saw Squire Gordon staring pointedly at him. Guiltily, the lawyer let the reins down again. Squire Gordon waved, and, mopping his brow, the lawyer waved back.

As we set off, I thought of how proud and happy I was to be living at such a fine place as Birtwick Park, where I worked for such a kind and well-respected master and mistress. They cared so much about horses, they made sure that other people's creatures were treated just as kindly as their own.

As we made our way home, the storm got much worse.

A rider on horseback approached from the other direction. He was a neighbour of the

Squire's and had just crossed the river. He warned us that the water was rising fast. We bid a hasty farewell and hurried as fast as we could to Cockington Bridge.

It was quickly getting dark. The wind howled around us as we were pelted with rain. The branches overhanging the road shook with a fury. It was frightening, but I knew I must continue and get John and Squire Gordon safely home. But first we had to get across the bridge.

By the time we arrived, it was completely dark. The river had risen so high that the bridge was completely covered with water. However, it appeared to be safe. The sturdy rails stood on each side, and the middle of the bridge rose above the water and looked quite dry. I waded out, but I stopped dead in my tracks when we approached the middle.

I was overcome with a feeling of unease. I didn't dare go any farther. I was sure that something was very wrong with the bridge. I started to back up as fast as I could.

Squire Gordon did not understand what was going on. 'Beauty, forward, go forward!' he shouted, shaking the reins. But I could not obey.

'Forward, Beauty! Are you mad?' he shouted, hitting me in the flank with the whip. It hurt, but I kept backing up.

The next thing I knew, John jumped down and grabbed the reins. 'Let's get out of this water. It's dry on the top,' he said, pulling me forward, forcing me to walk towards the middle of the bridge again.

But I knew something was terribly, terribly wrong, and I would not move any further. I would not go to the top of the hump, no matter how hard John pleaded or pulled.

'Come on, Beauty ... for me ...' John begged. Then he got angry. 'Come on!' he shouted. 'Move those feet! You crossed it this morning!'

John wasn't a bad man; he was a good man – but he didn't realize the danger he was putting us all in.

Finally John yanked me forward with all his might, and I was forced to move my feet. I had no choice. I'd tried my best to tell him, but I was raised to obey. I stepped forward, and John dragged me on to the hump bridge.

The next thing I knew, I plunged into the water. The bridge had collapsed underneath us!

I immediately scrambled backwards on to the bank. But poor John had lost his grip and was sucked into the raging river. He made a desperate grab for my reins, but I knew he wouldn't be able to hang on for long. The wet reins were slippery, and the turgid waters were threatening to sweep him away. Desperately, I dug my hoofs into the muddy bank. My neck ached from stretching so far, and the bit tore at my mouth.

There was nothing Squire Gordon could do but watch helplessly as I struggled to keep my footing and John held on for dear life.

Finally, after what seemed like for ever, I made one last mighty effort and pulled the drowning man closer to the bank. He grabbed hold of some plants and roots that grew there and Squire Gordon stepped in to pull him to solid ground. John lay curled in the mud, weeping and gasping for air, still clutching my reins in his hand.

Squire Gordon covered the shivering man with his coat.

I hurried back to Birtwick Park because I knew that John needed to get into a warm house and out of his wet clothes as soon as possible. When we reached the house, the door swung open and Mistress Gordon and Joe nearly flew out the door.

'I've been frantic!' Mistress Gordon said. 'Are you safe? Have you had an accident?'

'We almost lost John to the river,' replied the Squire.

'John!' gasped the mistress.

'I'll be all right, Mistress,' said the weak, still-shivering man as he tried to climb out of the back of the cart. 'Just need to look after the horse and –' He couldn't finish his sentence. It was obvious he was about to collapse. The Squire and Joe immediately came to his aid and supported him under each arm.

'No, you will not,' the mistress said firmly. 'You'll come inside at once.'

'But Black Beauty . . .' he protested weakly. 'He needs to be looked after.'

'I'll look after him, Uncle John,' Joe piped up.

'Do what I've shown you,' warned his weak but worried uncle.

Joe promised he would, and the Gordons led the tired head groom inside. I was exhausted too, soaking wet, and my breathing had not yet returned to normal. Steam rose from my coat as my overheated body met the cold night air. As Joe led me to the stable, I could overhear the Gordons talking together.

'What happened?' asked the mistress.

'Bless our Beauty. Far less than might have,' Squire Gordon said proudly.

Although I was tired, cold and wet, I still couldn't help but feel a thrill of pleasure at my master's compliment.

4

Sickness and Recovery

Back in the stable, Ginger and Merrylegs watched as Joe rubbed down my still-shaking legs.

'This will help you. I've seen Uncle John do it,' the boy said knowingly. I spotted my blanket and grabbed at it with my teeth. I couldn't wait to be warm again!

'No, Beauty,' said Joe, touching my still-steaming back. 'You're boiling hot! You won't want that rug tonight!'

But I *did* need the rug. I felt colder than I'd ever felt ... What I wouldn't have given for my blanket – for a heap of blankets!

But there was no way to communicate my need to the boy. He set my water bucket down in front of me, and I immediately began to drink.

'Thirsty?' asked the boy. 'It's good and cold.'

The icy water hit my stomach like a fierce kick in the gut, but I was very thirsty and drank it down as quickly as I could.

'I've never seen anybody drink so fast,' the young boy said in amazement.

I stood there, shaking and trembling, as Joe brought me another bucket of cold water.

'Drink up,' he said, setting it before me. Then he shut the door and left.

I knew I was in for a long, hard night without a blanket to keep me warm.

By the next morning, I was breathing heavily and could hardly open my eyes. I felt sore all over. My coat was matted with dried sweat, and I shivered and shook worse than ever. My stomach ached terribly. Perhaps if I lie down, I thought. Anything to ease the pain.

I was lying on the floor when I heard John's voice. I wanted to call out to him, but all I could manage was a low moan.

He was at my side in an instant. 'Oh, Lord,' he breathed. 'Beauty.' He quickly covered me with blankets. They felt wonderful!

I half-opened my eyes and saw Joe in the doorway with his eyes opened wide in shock.

'You're a stupid, stupid boy!' John growled. 'Where was his rug? I'll bet the water was cold, too!'

Little Joe's eyes filled with tears.

'Don't just stand there crying. Run to the house for the kettle!' John shouted at him. Joe disappeared.

John prepared a thin gruel of hot water and mash that he fed to me. Then I think I fell asleep.

I don't know how long I was ill. I only know it seemed like for ever. My ears were so sensitive, every little noise threatened to shatter my skull.

I remember waking to find Squire Gordon standing over me, his face sad.

'My poor Beauty,' he murmured. 'My good horse.'

He and John gave me some liquid medicine, which they poured through a tube inserted down into my stomach through my nose. It was horribly uncomfortable.

John stayed up with me all night long, just in case I needed any help.

It was very obvious how terrible Joe Green felt. Sometimes he would come into my stall and kiss my muzzle and whisper words of encouragement into my ear.

One day he came in, again begging me to get well. Suddenly I realized I felt a little stronger. I opened my eyes and lifted my head. Joe smiled at me excitedly. I wagged my head at him, as much like the way I did when I first arrived in the stable as my weak neck would allow.

'You're hungry?' the young boy asked, searching his pockets. 'I haven't got anything.'

I slowly and carefully rose to my feet. Joe looked at me in amazement, then ran out of the stall.

'Uncle John! Uncle John!' he cried excitedly. 'Come and see Black Beauty!'

Ginger looked over at me and we touched our noses together in greeting.

I was feeling better. Everything was going to be all right.

Pretty soon I was back to my normal self and I

was let out into the paddock for the first time since my illness. I whinnied anxiously, looking around for my friends.

Joe appeared, smiling happily at my improved state. I ran up to him, and for the first time, he didn't flinch.

'I brought you something this time,' he said, holding out a lump of sugar.

He climbed into the paddock with me and looked up into my eyes. 'Beauty, can you ever forgive me for letting you get ill?' he asked softly.

I nudged him playfully and moved away. I ran to the other side of the paddock and wagged my head at the boy, inviting him to play. Joe laughed out loud, his worries forgotten.

We played together in the paddock, chasing each other around and playing tag. Our little game was interrupted by John, calling his nephew back to work.

'Coming!' called Joe.

But I was not ready to give up my playmate so quickly. I chased the boy and walked around him, blocking his path.

'I can't play no more, Beauty,' he said and moved towards the gate.

I walked behind him and gave him a nudge. Joe stumbled forward. I was not about to let him ignore me!

'There's work I've got to do,' he said.

But I was not giving up. I circled him so he could not move. Joe looked at his uncle helplessly and threw his arms up in mock surrender.

'Why don't you take him down to the orchard?' his uncle called out.

Joe grinned happily at me.

At the orchard I was reunited with my friends, and we grazed happily under the apple trees once more.

But even as I was getting well, my mistress's health was failing her. She looked paler and paler and weaker and weaker. It worried me.

Meanwhile little Alfred Gordon stayed exactly the same – mean.

One day Alfred decided to pick on Merrylegs, chasing him around the meadow. As soon as Ginger and I realized what he was up to, we ran in between the boy and our little friend, forming a barrier to protect the pony. We stopped and circled the boy, trying to distract him. Merrylegs saw his chance and disappeared.

'Get away from me!' Alfred yelled. Suddenly he picked up a handful of stones and started throwing them at us, shouting, 'Leave me alone!' Ginger and I ran away as quickly as we could to avoid being hit, so Alfred chose his next target . . .

Joe arrived at the gate just in time to hear the two sisters scream.

'Master Alfred! Stop!' Joe shouted.

'Hurry, Joe! Get help!' yelled Jessica as she and her little sister dodged the stones.

'Help!' echoed little Molly.

Joe grabbed my halter and we started to run together back to the stables.

'Go faster!' shouted the terrified Jessica. 'Ride him!'

'Ride him?' Joe said to himself. 'But I . . . but I . . . I don't know how!'

However, the situation at hand called for immediate action. The brave boy quickly brought me over to the fence and climbed up on to my back. Then we set off on a wild ride back to the stables.

I did whatever I could to keep him from falling off my back – slowing, speeding up, swerving a little when I had to. It wasn't easy, but it worked. We made it back to the stableyard and John, with Joe clinging on to my back.

'Uncle John! Uncle John!' Joe shouted. 'It's Master Alfred! He's throwin' rocks at the horses! He's throwin' them at Miss Jessica and Miss Molly!'

John was furious. He mounted his horse at lightning speed and quickly set off for the orchard, his mouth set into a grim line.

Squire Gordon was just as angry as John had been. He brought his troublesome son into the stable and scolded him in front of the horses. Alfred hung his head in shame.

'You could have done some real harm to these animals,' he told the boy sternly.

'I'm sorry, sir,' Alfred said in a small, quiet voice. We had to strain to hear him.

'Don't say it to me,' his father reprimanded him. 'Say it to *them*.'

Alfred looked up at Ginger, Merrylegs and me, then quickly looked away. He looked miserable.

'I'm sorry, horses,' he mumbled.

'Louder. Like you mean it,' his father insisted.

'*I'm sorry, horses*,' he repeated loudly.

The boy was then sent inside to apologize to his little sisters.

The next morning I was awakened out of a sound sleep by the loud clanging of the stable bell. Alarmed, I scrambled to my feet, as did Ginger and Merrylegs.

I was quite surprised when my stall door flew open to reveal a brightly smiling Joe Green.

'Wake up, Beauty! You too, Ginger!' he called.

Gone was the scared, shy boy I had known. In his place was a self-confident young man who quickly and surely put on my driving bridle and saddle. The change in Joe was wonderful. He seemed to have grown an inch overnight.

5

Fire!

Ginger and I were off on a long trip. Our poor mistress was so ill that we needed to take her to a doctor, a specialist, who lived far away.

We rode far that first day and stopped for the night in a strange city. The Squire nearly had to carry his weak wife inside the hotel. Ginger and I were to stay in the hotel's stable, which was run by a nervous little man called an ostler. He had a crooked leg and wore a yellow striped vest.

When we were inside, John took çare of Ginger while Joe took care of me. They rubbed us down and cleaned us carefully. When the job was finished, Joe was sent up to the loft for our hay.

While he was gone, a coachman entered the stable leading a skittish horse. The man seemed surly and rude, puffing impatiently on his pipe.

'This stall still mine, old man?' he shouted at the ostler.

'Same as last night,' the little man said. 'Bring her along up here to rub her down. There's brushes and cloths –'

'Never mind that,' the coachman interrupted. 'She didn't do nothing but stand outside the shops all day.'

He quickly tied the horse and, muttering disagreeably, strode towards the hayloft ladder.

'I'll toss her some hay and then be off,' he said to no one in particular.

'You'll not take your pipe up there,' the ostler called after him.

'Yeah ... Yeah ...' the coachman replied gruffly.

However, I could see that the unpleasant man still had the pipe stem clenched between his teeth as he made his way up to the hayloft.

I realized that something was not quite right almost immediately. As John and Joe readied us for the night, I started getting very nervous and apprehensive. I was not sure exactly what was wrong.

The next thing I knew, I heard a crackling sound. It sounded loud and strange to me, but no one else seemed to notice it.

'Come along, chap,' John said, pulling on my rope and trying to lead me into my stall.

I couldn't understand why John couldn't hear the odd noise. I made a desperate lunge towards the stable doors.

John assumed that I was having trouble settling into the unfamiliar stable.

'Shh, shh, Beauty,' he said comfortingly. 'It's just for tonight.'

Just then Joe emerged from Ginger's stall.

'What's wrong?' he asked.

I kept hopping and lunging. I was trying to tell him that we had to get out of there!

But it was of no use. 'It's a strange stable,' John crooned to me comfortingly. 'I know, Beauty, I know.' Then he proceeded to force me into my stall.

Please! I silently begged.

'Calm yourself, now. Calm yourself,' he said. He looked around the stable but sensed nothing wrong.

I trembled as he patted me.

'It's secure enough in here,' he reassured me. 'What are you afraid of? You'll be all right.'

If only I could have made him understand. But I couldn't. It was just like the time at the river when I was forced to cross the bridge and John nearly drowned. He couldn't understand me then, and he couldn't understand me now.

John and Joe left, taking the lantern and shutting the big stable doors. We were left in the darkness. But not for long . . .

Pretty soon the air got very thick with smoke, and there were rushing sounds and sharp snapping and crackling noises. I had no idea what they were – if you've never heard or seen something before, how can you understand it?

But I did know that we were in danger.

The other horses began to stamp and cough as the smoke got thicker. What were we going to do? We were trapped!

Just then the big doors burst open and the ostler ran in. The fresh air cleared the smoke a bit, but the roaring sound got much, much worse. And then there was the man's panic.

'Oh, God! Oh, no! Oh, God!' he screamed. 'Fire! Oh, no! Now what? Oh, no!'

He was in a state of total hysteria as he frantically tried to untie the horses and lead them out. 'Come on! Don't stand there!' he screamed. 'You bloody fools! Come out!'

He entered my stall and started to claw at the knot tying my lead. Finally he managed to undo it. 'Come! You've got to come out! You've got to! Now!!!' he screamed at me, yanking on my lead, trying to pull me out of my stall by force. I was so terrified, I couldn't even move.

'Darn you!' he yelled at me, then gave up, running out the door.

'Fire! Fire! Fire!' he screamed.

Bells were clanging. People were yelling. The horrible roaring sound got louder and louder.

The next thing I knew, Joe Green was at my side. He was calm and cool and patted me constantly, calming me down. I was very surprised to see him. If I expected anybody at that moment, it would have been John.

'Let's get out of this smother,' Joe said. His quiet tone immediately soothed me. I trusted Joe and willingly followed him out of the stall.

But I immediately stopped in my tracks when I saw the leaping flames that surrounded us.

'Maybe if you don't have to look . . .' the quick-thinking boy suggested, covering my eyes with his scarf. Everything went black and I allowed myself to be led forward. All of a sudden I remembered my friend. Where was Ginger? I couldn't leave her! I had to find Ginger! I whinnied loudly, several times, but there was no answer.

Once we were outside in the fresh air, we met up with a worried John. Joe handed me over to him and ran back into the smoky building without a second thought.

'Joe!' shouted John, but the brave boy had already disappeared inside.

John tried to lead me further away from the burning stable, but I would not budge from the spot where I stood until I knew Ginger was safe. I whinnied over and over, hoping she could hear me.

I thought all was lost when I heard a horribly loud crash inside the burning building and the flames appeared to burn all the brighter. But the next moment Joe appeared, leading the blindfolded Ginger.

Ginger was safe. Thank God. My friend was safe. I didn't know what I would have done if anything had happened to her. She told me that if she hadn't heard me whinnying, she would never have had the courage to come out.

Squire Gordon patted Joe on the back and thanked him for his bravery.

The boy smiled proudly.

As the Squire and John inspected Ginger and me for damage, John bemoaned the fact that he once again had failed to heed my warning.

'If only I could learn to listen to them,' he murmured.

Even Mistress Gordon, sick as she was, leaned out of her hotel room window to check on our safety.

Ginger and I were lucky that night, but luck was not with our mistress.

The doctor said that her illness was very far advanced, and he ordered her to leave England for a warmer country at once. The news fell upon our household like the tolling of a death knell.

*

Soon it was time for the Gordon family to leave. Ginger and I carried our mistress and Alfred to the train station, and a tearful Jessica and Molly took one last ride in the dogcart with little Merrylegs. We watched sadly as the workmen loaded the family's possessions on to the train.

Squire Gordon lifted his ailing wife out of the carriage. She smiled weakly at John. 'Good-bye, John. God bless you,' she said sadly.

John bowed to her.

Jessica and Molly had a terrible time bidding farewell to their little pony. They kissed and hugged him, crying as if their hearts would break, until their impatient brother came over to hurry them away. As Alfred passed by the little pony, Merrylegs pinned back his ears and snapped at him. Startled, Alfred jumped out of the way of the angry pony, then turned to deliver his punishment.

'Into the train, Alfred,' said his father, with a warning tone in his voice.

Reluctantly, Alfred boarded the train.

It was time for the Squire to say good-bye. Horses can tell more by the voice than many men can. I knew that our master and John were very low-spirited. The Squire couldn't even look at his faithful head groom as he said good-bye and concentrated on patting my coat.

'I want to thank you, John,' he began, 'for your long and faithful service to my family . . .'

John's voice cracked as he responded. 'We shall never forget you, sir, and please God may we someday see Mistress Gordon back again and like herself . . .'

The master turned to clasp John's hand.

'We must keep up hope, sir,' John finished. The two men said their good-byes, and the Squire climbed aboard the train. It pulled out of the station in a puff of smoke.

That was the last time we would ever see our mistress. We drove home in a sad silence.

But it was not our home any more.

6

Earlshall Park

So we were to be parted. Ginger and I were sent off to the Earl of Wexmire's estate, and Merrylegs to the vicar's. The vicar promised he'd never sell Merrylegs. That was why our master let the vicar have him. Saying good-bye to that little pony was about as hard a thing as I've ever had to do.

In no time, Ginger and I also found ourselves miles away from everything dear and familiar. But at least we were still together.

Joe brought us to our new home, Earlshall Park, which was bigger and grander than Birt-wick Park – almost four times the size. But it wasn't half as pleasant. Two footmen in scarlet breeches and white stockings stood at the front door. It was a forbidding place.

Joe presented us to our new groom, a Mr York. He was impatient and imposing. I could immediately tell that Ginger did not take to him.

'Step up here,' he commanded. Ginger skittered away.

Joe spoke up. 'Black Beauty has a perfect temper,' he told the groom. 'But Ginger came to us snappish and suspicious. It was kind treatment that brought her back. My uncle says that if she were ill-used again, she'd likely give tit for tat.'

York pointed to a stall. 'Put the black one up in there,' he said.

'His name is Black Beauty,' declared Joe.

The groom didn't answer.

My new stall was clean, light and airy, but I was dismayed to see bars on the windows that kept me from looking out. It felt like a prison.

'Uncle John says you'd have to look long and hard to find a pair of horses better than these,' Joe said.

'Course they're not matched . . . but I suppose the Earl's idea is that they'll do for the country,' the groom said condescendingly.

Joe bit his lip, visibly upset by the man's rude attitude. He turned to me and caressed my head. 'If I could, you know I'd take you with me,' he whispered sadly. He sighed and took off my halter. 'I swear to you – someday, somehow, I'll be with you again.'

With that, he turned to leave. I didn't want my friend to go and stretched out my neck to him, wagging my head from side to side.

Joe tried to smile as he shut my stall door, but it was obvious he was just too sad.

I wondered if I ever would see that kind little fellow again.

There were two more grooms to meet. Their names were Reuben Smith and Ned Burnham. Reuben was a kind, older man. I could sense a sort of frustration in him from working under the harsh head groom, York.

The next day they harnessed Ginger and me to a fancy carriage and led us to the front of the mansion. The two footmen ceremoniously opened the front doors, and Lady Wexmire, a tall, proud-looking woman dressed in finery such as I'd never seen before, the Earl and their son, Lord George, emerged.

The three descended the stairs and came to look at their new horses. Lord George seemed especially taken with Ginger. 'Look at the long legs on the chestnut. What a hunter she'd make. She could fly over the jumps,' he said.

I immediately noticed that he did not refer to Ginger by name, nor did he give her a new one. It was to be this way our entire time at Earlshall Park. I was 'the black horse' and Ginger was 'the chestnut mare'.

Lady Wexmire was very upset that we were not wearing the bearing reins that my old master so despised. 'York, you must put these horses' heads higher,' she insisted.

Lord Wexmire protested, 'They're not accustomed to the bearing reins, my dear. Their groom said they've never used the bearing reins with either of them ... It would be safer to bring them up by degrees.'

'Pish, posh,' replied Lady Wexmire. 'These animals aren't fit to be seen. One notch tighter won't kill them, will it?'

'As you wish, my lady,' replied York.

Although the reins were only shortened by one hole, every little bit makes a difference. It added a lot of pressure to my mouth. And later that day, when we had to pull the carriage up a steep hill, we had a great deal of difficulty and got winded very quickly.

The bearing reins were just as terrible as Squire Gordon described. Ordinarily I would have put my head forward and taken the carriage up with all my strength, but no, I had to pull with my head up now. It took all the spirit out of me. Pain shot down my back and legs.

No, Earlshall Park was not at all a pleasant place to live – if a horse may have an opinion.

Every day Lady Wexmire insisted that our reins be shortened another notch. Every notch was like being choked . . . a little more . . . and a little more . . . I felt worse for Ginger than I felt for myself. But she said she could stand it, provided it didn't get any worse.

However, the worst was yet to come.

One day as Ned and Reuben were harnessing us to the fancy carriage to take Lady Wexmire to visit the Duchess of Buford, York flew into the stable in a rage. His face was as red as the coat he was wearing.

'Ned! Reuben! What the devil!' he shouted.

'Why isn't the carriage at the door yet?' Then he turned to Reuben and angrily demanded, 'Are you drinking again, man?'

Reuben was obviously quite offended by this question. 'Drinking!' he shouted. 'I haven't! Not in months!'

'Drinking or not drinking, you'll get yourself sacked if you don't get those horses harnessed! Go! Go! Go!' he shouted, hitting the groom.

Reuben, looking as if he might explode, returned to the harnessing. When we were finally ready, York climbed on board and snapped his whip, driving to the entrance at breakneck speed.

Lady Wexmire was clad in an even more extravagant outfit, complete with a large plumed hat. She was furious.

'For God's sake, York,' she said shrilly. 'Are you never going to get those horses' heads up? Raise them at once!'

'As you wish, my lady,' the groom replied.

'Quickly!' she said in a warning tone.

York hurried over to me and fixed the reins so tightly I could feel my eyes bulge. Ginger was next – and she shook her head up and down angrily. As soon as York took her rein off in order to shorten it, she saw her chance and reared up, knocking the groom to the ground. Kicking and plunging, she inadvertently landed a hard kick below my knee, then she kicked over the carriage pole that separated us, falling over. York held her down as Reuben and Ned ran up to help.

'Unbuckle the black horse!' York barked furiously. 'Get over here and unscrew the carriage pole!'

When they cut me free from Ginger and the carriage, I was overexcited and broken into a sweat. My leg was in terrible pain. But I couldn't help wondering what was going to happen to Ginger.

Reuben led me away and shut me up in my stall. The saddle was still on and the reins were unbearably tight. My leg hurt where Ginger had kicked me. My head was strained up and there was nothing I could do about it. If ever in my life I wanted to kick somebody, it was at that very moment.

Ginger was led back into the stable. She looked terrible – battered, bruised and in shock. York yelled for blankets for Ginger and hot water and lotion for me. As the grooms scurried off, he stepped into my stall. I was still quite agitated. He grabbed at the rein and snapped it. 'Stand!' he commanded sharply.

So I stood – *hard* – on his foot.

York hobbled out of my stall, ordering Reuben to take care of me instead.

'As you wish, Mr York,' said the groom, mimicking his boss while trying hard not to smile.

Reuben removed the saddle and bridle and bathed my hurt leg, grumbling to himself, 'It's her own silly fault if she misses her tea party . . . Not yours . . . not mine, either. It's mad enough to drive us all back to drink.'

Little did I know how ominous those seemingly innocent words really were.

7

The Accident

Once Ginger's bruises healed, she became Lord George's riding horse. He'd wanted her all along. He was a hard rider and careless of his horse, but better a tender back than the eternal vexations of those bearing reins, or so Ginger and I thought. I, on the other hand, continued to be subject to my lady's whims.

She even had Reuben bring me into the house so she could paint my portrait!

One day Reuben was sent to town to have the brougham − a small light carriage − repaired. The ride was rough because the roads were newly mended and littered with stones. Reuben complained the whole way.

The carriage maker and his assistant inspected the carriage, telling Reuben that it would need a lot more work than the coat of paint Lady Wexmire had requested.

Reuben thought a minute, then put a saddle on me. 'Keep the horse for me, will you?' he asked the assistant. 'Leave him saddled.' Then he added in a mocking tone, 'I daren't be late.'

'Where are you going, Reuben?' asked the carriage maker.

'I'll be back,' Reuben said over his shoulder.

We all watched as he made his way towards the tavern. I was surprised – from what Reuben had told Mr York, he had given up drinking. The carriage maker and his assistant exchanged a sad look.

Several hours later I was fast asleep in the stable when I was awakened by a bellowing voice. I looked around frantically. I was the only horse left there.

'Where is everybody?' Reuben shouted as he staggered inside.

The assistant had been sleeping nearby on a bale of hay. He sat up groggily and lit a lantern.

'Why ain't he saddled?' the drunken groom

slurred. 'I specifically told you specifically to keep him saddled. I'm due back!'

'But, Mr Smith, it's been hours!' the assistant protested.

Reuben tossed the saddle on to my back. But when he tried to tighten the girth, he yanked the saddle right off my back and on to the floor.

The carriage maker's assistant picked the saddle up but did not hand it back to the groom.

'Are you sure you should be riding, Mr Smith?' he questioned as politely as the situation warranted.

'"Are you sure you should you be riding, Mr Smith?"' mimicked the groom. 'Just put it on,' he growled.

The assistant was obviously intimidated by Reuben. He saddled me up, then led me to the groom. As I walked, my foot made a strange clacking sound.

'Listen,' he said to Reuben, holding up my left front leg and wiggling the shoe. 'There's a loose nail in his shoe.'

'Forget the bloody shoe!' Reuben roared and dragged me out into the night.

*

After a couple of failed attempts to get on my back, in which he insisted I was moving away from him but I was, in fact, standing perfectly still, Reuben next tried to use the mounting block. However, he ended up sitting backwards. 'Where's your darn head?' he asked my tail angrily, then slid off. It would have been funny if the situation wasn't so grim.

He finally pulled himself up, and we took off into the dark night.

I ran as fast as I could, but Reuben kept urging me to speed up. Then, losing his balance, he shouted 'Ho!' in panic. 'Ho' is the command to stop, so I did. Reuben fell out of the saddle and slid to the ground in a heap.

'Damn well-trained horse . . .' he slurred. 'I won't be saying *that* again.'

When he got back on, he had a tree branch in his hand that he used as a whip. 'Giddyup! Move! Move!' he shouted.

We turned on to the turnpike – the newly paved road Reuben had complained about on the way into town. The stones were big and sharp, but he continued running me, faster and faster. My mouth was foaming and my shoe was getting looser and looser. But he was too drunk to notice. He whipped me harder and dug into my sides with his sharp spurs.

Finally the shoe fell off. I could feel my naked hoof crack and splinter. I stumbled – then I fell hard on to my knees. Reuben was flung off my back and flew for quite a distance before he crashed to the ground. It was a bone-crunching fall.

Quickly I got to my feet and limped off the rocky road on to a patch of soft grass. I stared at Reuben. I saw him attempt to move, so I knew he was alive. He groaned heavily.

I was in too much pain to move. I looked around me. The road was empty. The night was quiet and still. I could see the spire of an old church rising above the trees and an empty moonlit field.

How could something so terrible happen on such a calm, sweet night?

As I stood there, other nights returned to me. I was brought back to the nights of long ago when I used to lie beside my mother and she would nuzzle me gently before I fell asleep. What wonderful, content times those were!

But memories couldn't rescue me for long. Reuben Smith still lay in the middle of the road where he fell, and there was nothing for me to do but wait, and watch, and listen.

It was not until the next morning that help arrived. I thought I heard the sound of cart wheels, so I whinnied out loud. Imagine my surprise and happiness when Ginger answered me!

Soon she turned the bend and there she was, pulling York and Ned in a dogcart.

I nickered in greeting but could not move forward.

The two men jumped out of the cart and surveyed the sad scene of last night's accident.

They lifted the softly groaning Reuben on to the back of the cart.

Ned immediately assumed that I had thrown the groom. 'Who'd have thought the black horse would throw anybody?' Ned asked in a frightened voice.

'But I never saw one that didn't run for home,' York replied thoughtfully.

When they approached me, they could see the damage that was done to my knees – they were bloody and raw.

'God, look at his knees,' Ned said.

York tried to lead me forward. When I limped, he lifted up my hoof.

'This darn hoof's torn to shreds,' York exclaimed.

'Reuben should have stopped when the shoe came loose,' Ned said.

York glowered at him. 'Why do you think he didn't?' he asked angrily.

'But he swore he'd never drink again!' Ned protested.

'Think again,' York said, taking his handkerchief out and binding my splintered hoof with it.

We returned to Earlshall Park very, very slowly. Ginger pulled Reuben in the dogcart, and Ned guided me. Every step was agony.

My knees were a painful mess. York worked on them carefully, cleansing the wounds, dousing them with many different kinds of medicine, and finally cauterizing them with a hot iron.

The joints weren't damaged, but my knees would always be blemished. My recovery was long and painful.

Reuben had hurt his head and his arm pretty badly. Although he never said a word, I could tell from the look on his face whenever he looked at me that he felt very, very sorry for what he had done.

I was turned out to a small pasture to wait out my recovery. As much as I enjoyed the liberty and the sweet grass, I didn't like being alone. I missed Ginger.

From my pasture, I had a clear view of the steeplechase. One day I watched a pack of horses and riders furiously jumping the fences, streams and hedges. And then, in the middle of them all, I spotted Ginger! I could tell that Lord George, who was on her back, was forcing her to keep up with the riders in the front of the pack. Ginger did not disappoint him. They came in among the first three.

I was very happy for her. But afterwards, even from a distance, Ginger appeared to be breathing very heavily. Was something wrong with her?

I couldn't believe my eyes. Lord Wexmire and York were bringing Ginger into my little pasture! Excitedly I ran over to greet my old friend. Ginger ran towards me as well but then stopped

67

to cough. I touched noses with her. We had a joyful reunion.

I was right. Something *was* wrong with Ginger. She told me that after the race, Lord Wexmire came over to congratulate his son. But when he heard Ginger cough, he was so angry that he wouldn't even shake his son's hand.

Lord George hadn't bothered to train her before the race and had broken her. She couldn't breathe properly now.

Lord Wexmire and York watched us, and I could hear him say to York, 'My friend thought his favourite horses would find a good home here . . . And now look at them . . . ruined.'

'A twelve-month run should bring the mare's wind back, my lord,' York protested.

'But the black one will have to be sold. I'll not have knees like that in my stables,' said Lord Wexmire.

Then he turned and marched off.

I knew I had to go, but I didn't expect it to happen so fast. One morning they took me away – so suddenly that Ginger and I didn't even have a chance to say good-bye.

8

A Job Horse and His Drivers

My next home, if it could be called such a sweet name as 'home', was at the job horse stables. The job boss was a rough man who didn't have a kind bone in his body. He even harnessed his horses cruelly and carelessly. But I could not complain. I was a 'job horse' now – let out to anyone who would hire me.

Before this I had always been driven by people who at least knew how to drive. But not any more. I could separate the drivers into three categories. There were the tight-rein drivers, like the skinny man who insisted on keeping an uncomfortably hard hand on my reins, yanking on my mouth constantly. He kept telling his companion he was 'holding me up' – just as if horses were not made to hold themselves up.

Then there were those who employed the steam-engine style of driving. People like this think that just because they paid for using us, we should go as far and as fast as they want us to. They forget that we're made of flesh and blood.

The red-haired young man who insisted on galloping me up a terribly steep hill was such a driver. He whipped me when I didn't go fast enough for him, then galloped me up another hill.

Then there were the loose-rein drivers. I was hired for the day by a family, and the father was so engrossed in his surroundings, pointing out ducks and trees and the countryside in general, that he paid little attention to his driving. I began to get nervous, especially when we went around a corner so sharply that the carriage almost tipped over. The family thought it was great fun and hooted with laughter.

'Do it again, Dad!' the son shouted.

The road we took next was rocky, and the driver didn't seem to notice, much less make sure that we drove on the smoothest part. I immediately picked up a stone in one of my front feet. It hurt terribly, and I began to limp. Any good driver would have immediately been able to tell that something was wrong. But this man kept on talking and laughing. No one noticed the fact that I was in pain. They only noticed that I wasn't going as quickly as I had before. The father shook the reins impatiently.

'Stop dillydallying!' he said. 'Get a move on there!' I couldn't help it – I continued to slow down. Then the family spotted a hot air balloon rising in the distance.

'Hurry or we'll miss them!' the son shouted.

'Go! Go! Go!' shouted the father, cracking the whip across my back.

The whip stung, and I was forced to quicken my pace. But it still wasn't fast enough for them. The whip was cracked over and over.

I lost my balance and went crashing to my knees . . . again.

I was for sale again. At the horse fair, I saw horses everywhere I looked – beautiful horses in their prime, strings of wild, untamed ones, ponies no bigger than Merrylegs, and lots and lots of horses that had obviously once been handsome and highbred but had been misused in some way or another – just like me. There were also horses in even worse shape than we were – overworked and dejected-looking creatures.

And the people! There were so many people there. Untrustworthy sellers, buyers looking for a bargain, screaming children and harried parents.

I stood all day, hitched to a long line of horses. Several men looked us over, but most moved on quickly.

The dealer was getting a little desperate. A man with a hard face stepped up to inspect me, looking in my mouth and pulling on my eyelids, but he stopped when he got to my knees.

'What happened?' he asked.

'He took a spill in the stall. Them marks is just scratches,' the man lied.

The hard-faced man clearly did not believe him but continued examining me. His touch was rough. I could tell from his manners that he would not be a very kind master. I raised my head higher and higher to get away from him.

That was when I saw him. I couldn't believe my eyes, but I was staring right at my dear friend from Birtwick Park – Joe Green! He was taller and older than I remembered, but it was him. He walked right by without noticing me.

I had to get away from the rough man. I pulled away from him, bobbing and shaking my head. But the persistent fellow took this as an invitation to wrestle with me. By the time I wrested my head away from him to whinny, Joe was too far away.

I was heartbroken. The hard-faced man tried to get me into a headlock, but I struggled against him.

'Lively one, ain't he?' asked the anxious horse dealer. 'No horse with bad knees could hop like that, could he? He's yours for fifty pounds.'

'Fifty pounds!' the man said incredulously. He laughed a cruel laugh and finally let me go. 'You're off your rocker, mate' were his parting words as he stalked off.

I anxiously scanned the crowd for Joe . . . but he was gone.

The dealer was next approached by a pleasant-looking man. 'I'll give twenty-five for him,' he said.

'Twenty-five pounds?' the dealer asked, as if he couldn't believe what he had just heard. I could tell he was only pretending to be offended. 'For *him*?'

The man nodded. The dealer hesitated for a moment. 'Say twenty-six and you'll have him.'

But this man knew what he wanted. 'Twenty-five ten and not another penny,' he said.

The dealer nodded morosely. 'Done.'

My new owner took my halter and led me off the fairgrounds and into the streets of London. I had no idea where I was going or what was going to happen to me. There were people, people everywhere – people pushing and running and shoving me on all sides. The smell was awful. The noise was deafening. Where were the trees? Where was the grass? How could there be so many faces in the world?

We passed through a dark tunnel crowded with people who seemed to have no homes and down a narrow, rather poor-looking street. The stable was dark and dank and tiny. There was a carriage inside. This was to be my new home.

So here I was . . . with a man who seemed assured enough with a horse, but whose temper I couldn't read, stuck in this awful place. What was going to happen to me?

74

Farmer Grey meets the newborn.

The Squire and
Mrs. Gordon

Black Beauty and Joe Green

Mean Alfred Gordon chases his sisters and Merrylegs.

Ginger and Merrylegs, Black Beauty's dearest friends.

John Manly and Joe care for the ailing Black Beauty.

Joe Green leads Ginger out of the stable fire to safety.

Jessica and Molly bid a sad farewell to Merrylegs.

Lord Wexmire

Lady Wexmire

Ginger rebels against
the bearing reins.

A drunken Reuben Smith
falls out of the saddle.

Jerry and Dolly Barker groom their new horse.

The Barker family brushes Black Beauty.

Black Beauty's first day pulling the cab.

Black Beauty and Jerry wait
in the cold for a fare.

Pulling the grain wagon, Black
Beauty collapses from exhaustion.

Black Beauty and Joe Green —
reunited at last.

In my dreams . . . I rear giddily, just for the joy of it.

Just then the stable door flew open, and in ran a woman, a boy who looked to be about twelve and a little girl. They all looked at me expectantly. I backed away from them.

'What's wrong with him, Jerry?' the woman asked.

'He's frightened, Polly,' the man replied.

Jerry pulled me into the light.

'Frightened?' asked Polly. 'What made you buy him?'

Jerry ran his fingers through my mane.

'Poor horse,' said the little girl. 'Look at his hair. It's all in a mess.'

Jerry nodded. 'Bring me a brush, Dolly,' he told the little girl. Then he smiled at his wife. 'Don't worry,' he said.

The son, Harry, filled my stall with hay.

Dolly returned with the brush and handed it to her father. He began to brush my mane. Dolly wanted to help and noisily dragged a stool to my side. The sudden noise scared me and I jumped.

'Dolly! No!' shouted Polly.

'Come on, Dolly, but quietly,' said Jerry. 'Give him a chance.'

Their careful work began to relax me. It was

wonderful to be cared for again. It reminded me of the olden times.

'He's so soft,' whispered Dolly, stroking my mane.

'Yes, he is,' her father whispered back. He turned to his wife. 'Help us out, Polly,' he said.

She slowly approached and began brushing my side. Harry soon joined in.

'What shall we call him?' the son asked.

'Jack — after the old one,' suggested the father.

'He's much blacker than Jack,' his wife pointed out. 'When he's cleaned, his colour comes up lovely.'

'Oh . . . seeing something in him, are you, Polly?' Jerry teased.

'I didn't say that,' she retorted.

'We'll call him Black because he is . . . Jack after the old one . . . and Black Jack all together because the odds are stacked . . . against us both,' explained Jerry.

Polly shook her head and smiled.

'Black Jack,' said Harry, testing the name. I nuzzled him. I was glad to have part of my name back.

*

Dolly and Jerry braided my mane and my tail. My coat glowed from the brushing. I looked up at Jerry Barker and his family. They seemed like a lovely family — all very fond of each other and very happy. All at once I had hope. It's good people that make good places.

But still I wondered what tomorrow would bring.

9

The Cab

Tomorrow brought work. Jerry was a cabdriver and I was to pull the cab. At first I was nervous on the busy streets of London, with the hurrying pedestrians and carriages swinging close by. But Jerry's manner was much like Farmer Grey's and John Manly's, and his quiet soothings calmed me down. He had a light, expert touch with a horse. I was thankful that there were no bearing reins!

I could hardly stand the hurry and the chaos and the crowds. If it hadn't been for Jerry's voice, I don't know what I would have done.

We drove down a side street and approached the cabstand for the first time. A number of cabs were lined up side by side, waiting for fares.

'Halloo!' shouted the first cabbie in line. 'Have you got a good one, Jerry?' he asked, looking me over.

'Bah! He's too black!' grumbled the second. 'Be good for a funeral.'

We pulled up at the back of the line. Just then another fellow noticed my braids. 'Plaits in his mane and tail?' He laughed. 'What, are you driving in a parade this afternoon, Jerry?'

The other cabbies joined in the laughter.

'He wanted to be pretty for his first day,' said Jerry.

'He did, did he?' asked the second cabbie. The first cabbie took off with a passenger, still laughing.

I was lucky once again. I found out just what a kind master Jerry was when he climbed down from the cab and put some sticks under the shafts, the two long pieces of wood that were attached to the cab on either side of me. This eased the weight on my back. I was very grateful.

'This will take some of the weight off you, Black, old Jack, old boy,' he said.

The second cabbie got a fare and we moved farther up the line.

Jerry stroked my shoulders in gentle little circles. It felt very nice, and I relaxed almost immediately.

Just then an older man called from the other side of the street. 'That the new one, Jerry?' he asked.

'It is, Guv,' Jerry answered. I later found out that the man's name was Grant. Because he had been at the cabstand longer than anyone else, he took it upon himself to settle matters and stop disputes. And so he was known as Governor Grant or 'Guv' for short.

The cab in front of us took off, and I was next in line. Another cab pulled in to our right too quickly. It gave me a bit of a start. The man was rough-looking, and his horse looked tired and overworked. Jerry could tell that the close proximity made me tense and he knew what to do. He continued to stroke me and said quietly, 'Don't worry, old chap. Don't worry.' His calming touch and his quiet tone gave me confidence.

Governor Grant, who had been watching the entire scene, pulled away, calling, 'He's the right sort for you, Jerry. Good luck with him.'

'Thank you, Governor,' Jerry called back.

Just then two wild-looking young men made their way quickly towards our cab. They were in such a hurry that they pushed aside a woman and knocked over her cart and didn't even pause to help her. One jumped up into the cab. The other shouted, 'Here, cabbie! Look sharp! Put on the steam, will you, and get us to Victoria Station for the one o'clock train. It will mean a shilling extra.'

'We'll take you there but at the regular pace, sir,' Jerry said evenly. It was obvious that he was not rushing for anybody or any reason.

The mean-looking cabbie to my right lost no time throwing open the door of his cab, calling out, 'I'm your man, gentlemen! I'll get you there on time!'

The two young men scrambled into his cab.

'It's against his conscience to work his horse into a sweat,' the cabbie said, looking over at Jerry. 'But it ain't against mine!'

With a slash of his whip, the cab took off as quickly as possible, with the cabbie shouting, 'Make way! Make way! Coming through!' The cab teetered as the horse struggled through the streets. It was a distressing sight to see.

'Easy, Black,' Jerry said. Then he turned to

the woman whose cart had been overturned. 'Are you all right, Dinah?' he asked.

'I am. Thanks, Jerry,' she replied.

Jerry took one last look at the departing cab. The horse was clearly already winded, and the cab rocked back and forth as if it would tip over.

'Bonkers. All of 'em,' he said, shaking his head. 'Marbles and conkers.'

I soon became a good cab horse. I learned to pull the cab on city streets slick with rain and not lose my balance, and to relax during what could sometimes be long waits at the cabstand. In time I became calmer and more confident on the busy streets of London. Jerry made it all as easy as he possibly could. He was as thoughtful and patient a master as I'd ever known.

The workweek was hard, but Sundays were always our day of rest. Jerry would take me out to the doorway of the small stable and clean me carefully.

But one Sunday morning was different. Polly hurried out. 'Dinah Brown's mother is in a bad way,' she told her husband, looking worried.

'Oh . . .' replied Jerry. 'Poor Dinah.'

'She can't even go to her,' Polly continued. 'The place is in the country and there aren't any trains on Sunday.'

Jerry knew exactly what his wife was asking him. 'The horse is tired, Polly,' he said. 'I'm tired, too. It's our one day of rest.'

'But oughtn't we . . .' began Polly.

Jerry joined in and they both finished her sentence. '. . . treat folks the way we'd like to be treated?' Polly laughed.

'You're giving me my Sunday sermon early today, are you?' Jerry asked.

'I know that if my mother was dying . . .' Polly said, looking sad.

Jerry sighed. 'If I could borrow a lighter cart from somebody . . . it would make a wonderful difference to the horse.'

Obviously Polly had a plan. The next thing I knew, the butcher came round the corner wheeling his light carriage.

'Here comes Butcher Braydon now to lend you his trap,' Polly said with a smile.

Jerry laughed. 'You're a clever woman, Poll,' he said.

'You need looking after, too,' she continued. 'I'll make you a sandwich.' She turned and headed into the house. 'Won't take a minute,' she called back over her shoulder.

Jerry smiled.

It was a beautiful day, and I rather liked the idea of a jaunt in the country.

Autumn was in the air, but there was still a bit of warmth left. The carriage was light and easy to pull, especially compared to the heavy four-wheeled cab. It was fantastic to get out of the city.

When we arrived at the Brown family's small cottage, I noticed some cows grazing in a small meadow. Dinah suggested that Jerry let me loose with them.

'If the cows won't mind,' replied Jerry. 'It would be a rare treat for him to have a turnout.'

'You're too good with horses to be a cabbie, Jerry,' said Dinah. 'You ought to be a coach-man.'

Jerry smiled. 'If only . . . ah . . . dreams . . .' he said, handing her her last parcel. 'Run to see your mother, Dinah.'

'Thank you, Jerry,' said Dinah as she hurried inside. 'I don't know how to repay you . . .

Jerry smiled and led me to the small pasture.

It felt so good to be free! Grass! Not a cobble-stone in sight! I didn't know what to do first – roll, run or gobble up the beautiful green stuff . . . So I did them all.

I hadn't been in a meadow for a very long time. Jerry smiled at my antics. He sat beneath a tree, eating the sandwich that Polly had made for him. I cantered a bit, then skidded to a stop in front of my master. Jerry laughed. I wanted to play. Lunging forward, I grabbed the sand-wich out of his hand.

'Black!' he cried. 'What the . . .' He stood up and began to run after me. This was such fun! I trotted in a stiff circle around him. It was just like the days at Birtwick Park, playing with my friend Joe Green, except, of course, I was much older and stiffer now. Jerry and I continued our little game, chasing each other until he collapsed on the grass. I decided to be nice and returned his sandwich, dropping it on his heaving chest. Jerry raised his head. 'Right, thanks,' he said, looking at the mangled wet sandwich.

I dropped my head to graze beside him.

'Don't mind me.' Jerry laughed. 'You feel free. Eat . . .'

The rattling of a passing carriage made him look up. It was a handsome carriage, and the family inside the coach looked healthy and happy. The horses were well kept and driven properly. But Jerry seemed to be paying the most attention to the coachman and footmen.

I wondered what he was thinking.

When we were back in London that night, Polly helped Jerry clean and feed me as he told her about our day in the country. 'Dinah said she'd put in a word for me,' he told her.

'Did she?' asked Polly.

'Aw, Polly,' he said with a sigh. 'You know they wouldn't hire the likes of me as a groom on that estate – never mind the coachman. But it was a pretty sight.'

'We can always dream,' his wife replied.

'That's what I said, isn't it, Black?' he asked, patting me. 'If we don't have hope, we don't have nothing, eh, old chap?'

I silently agreed.

The seasons quickly changed and soon it was winter. Jerry made sure that whenever we waited at the cabstand I was covered with a warm blanket. One cold day I was eating the hay he had set out for me when a shabby-looking cab pulled up beside us. The old worn-out chestnut mare that was pulling it looked so sad and pitiful with her scraggly coat and sticking-out bones. The driver did not even cover her with a blanket, despite the chilly wind that was blowing. Her legs looked weak and wobbly. A gust of wind blew a bit of my hay in her direction and she stretched out her long, thin neck to grab it. She ate the bit of food eagerly, then looked at me, hoping for more. I stared into her dull, hopeless-looking eyes and looked at the white streak down her forehead. All of a sudden I knew who it was. Ginger!

I nickered in greeting, and she nickered back, then coughed. I stepped closer and we touched noses. How she had changed! Her spirit was broken, and she still had her terrible cough. I asked her why she didn't stand up for herself any more. She said she didn't have the strength. She never got rest on Sundays like I did. Her life was work, work, work, seven days a week. Her hard life made her realize that it's no use fighting — men are strongest.

Just then her driver came to drag her away.

She turned and told me I was the only friend she ever had. She stumbled away from me, unresisting, gazing at me as long as she could.

Her driver climbed up to the driver's seat of the cab, slashed her with his whip, and drove off.

Watching my dear friend leave, I felt as if my heart would break.

Sometimes when the long day of pulling the cab was over, back in the stables I would fall into a deep sleep and dream. I often dreamed of Ginger and Merrylegs chasing each other through the apple trees and up the hill in the glow of the setting sun.

Not many days later, it seemed like Jerry was getting ill. He sneezed loudly as we stood on the cab line in the rain. He was soaking wet, as was I. He threw a tarpaulin over me to protect me from the weather.

Then a cart passed by our stand. In it lay a dead horse – a chestnut horse with a long, thin neck and a white streak down the forehead.

It was Ginger. Poor Ginger. At least her troubles were over.

10

Another Good-bye

The rain continued all day, and Jerry got iller and iller. That evening, as Harry and Jerry fed and cleaned me, Polly noticed his coughing and sneezing.

'You didn't catch a chill today, did you, Jerry?' she asked.

'I'm all right,' he replied, rubbing me down.

'You couldn't stand another cough like you had last year,' Polly said worriedly.

'I'll be all right,' he tried to assure her.

Polly left and returned with my pan of mash, with Dolly close behind.

'Dolly, take your daddy inside for a cup of tea,' she told her daughter.

'Come with me, Daddy,' Dolly instructed her father.

'As soon as Black Jack's had his rub-down,' Jerry protested.

'Harry knows how to do that, don't you, Harry?' asked Polly.

'Course I do,' replied the boy.

Jerry handed his son the piece of burlap sacking he was using, saying, 'Make sure he's all dry, son.'

'I will,' the boy replied.

Polly gave me my pan of mash as Harry rubbed me down briskly. Dolly took her father's hand. As they left the stable, Jerry sneezed again. Polly turned round and watched her husband anxiously.

Cold nights were hard for an ailing man such as Jerry Barker, but a man must make a living and support his family. So we worked on the chilliest of nights to bring in the money.

But there was only so much a sick and tired soul could take. One evening we stood outside an elegant house in the falling snow, waiting for a fare to emerge from a party in a fashionable part of town. We had been asked to arrive at nine o'clock, and Jerry was always punctual. The clock struck ten . . . and then eleven. Jerry had covered me with a blanket and now pulled it higher to cover my neck.

'Gentlemen love their card parties, Black,' he said, patting my neck. 'But they'll be out presently. You'll see.'

He paced the pavement to keep warm, stamping his feet to bring back the feeling into his numb toes. He tried to beat his arms for warmth, but he started to cough and had to stop. He pulled open the cab door and sat inside. But nothing could keep the sick man warm.

As the clock struck midnight, the street lamps shut off, leaving us in darkness.

A while later, Jerry rang the bell of the house. A butler opened the door. I could barely hear Jerry's voice, it was so hoarse.

'Begging your pardon. I was engaged to come round at nine o'clock. As it's now after midnight, I thought perhaps the gentlemen wouldn't want –'

The butler wouldn't let him finish. 'Oh, yes,' he said brusquely. 'You'll be wanted soon enough. The party's nearly over.'

Jerry nodded. There was nothing else that he could do. The butler shut the door, and Jerry returned to the cab, adjusting my blankets. He suddenly had a terrible coughing fit. When he was through, he slid his freezing hands under my blanket to warm them.

We waited some more. Finally the door to the house opened and light spilled out on to the darkened street. Jerry looked up and stiffly got to his feet. Two gentlemen drunkenly hollered good-night to their host and made their way to the cab. They jumped in and slammed the door shut. Jerry slowly removed my blankets, his hands stiff with cold.

'Get a move on, man!' one of the men shouted. 'It's *freezing*.'

'Just a moment, sir,' Jerry whispered slowly and politely. I could tell that he would have liked to say a lot more to the men, but he held himself back.

Even the slightest movement was an effort for my master. He hardly seemed to be able to get any breath and had to stop to cough a couple of times.

We were both numb with the cold. I was afraid that I was going to stumble. But somehow we got the gentlemen to their houses. They never apologized for keeping us waiting so long.

*

It was late the next morning before anyone came. I waited eagerly for Jerry and my breakfast. But it was only Harry, who very quietly carried my hay to me. He was very still and didn't whistle or sing. I didn't know why until Governor Grant poked his head into the stable.

'I didn't want to trouble them at the house, Harry, but . . . how's your dad?' he asked.

'It's in his lungs, sir,' the young boy said, his voice trembling.

Governor Grant shook his head sadly. 'I'm sorry, my boy.'

'The doctor said it'll turn one way or the other tonight,' Harry explained.

'Keep your chin up, Harry, and help your mum. If there's any rule that good men should overcome bad things, he'll come through it,' Governor Grant said.

Then he turned and left.

I anxiously awaited the doctor's news, staring at his horse and buggy that were parked alongside me in the stable.

Suddenly I heard shouting in the house. 'He'll get well!' Harry and Dolly yelled happily.

'Hush, children,' I heard Polly scold them. 'Harry! Dolly! Quiet! Your father's still very ill!'

'But he's going to get better!' little Dolly exclaimed.

There were some muffled words and footsteps. The next thing I heard was Polly thanking the doctor outside the stable. They came in.

'You won't be thanking me next time,' the doctor said grimly. 'If he wants to live to be an old man, he's got to give up the cab work ...' He led his horse out of the stable and Polly followed. I couldn't hear any more of the conversation.

I was awfully glad that Jerry was alive. But I couldn't help wondering, if Jerry could no longer drive a cab, what was to happen to me?

Harry walked me on a lead line down the street from the house. Confused, I tried to turn the corner towards the cabstand.

'No, Black,' said the boy, 'we're not going to work today.' He turned me round and we headed back towards home. 'We're just stretching your old legs, old Black Jack.'

As we turned down their street, Dinah swept past us, a huge smile on her face. Harry and I both wondered why. We turned to go into the stable.

Soon Dolly came bursting out of the house. 'Harry! Harry!' she shouted. 'Dinah says we're going to live in the country! There's a cottage and cows and chickens. Daddy's going to drive coaches. There's an estate and they have horses and coaches there! He'll never have to drive a cab ever again!' The two children embraced happily.

I quietly watched the joyful children. Never to drive a cab again? This was heavy news to me. I knew I wouldn't be going with them. I wasn't fit for an estate.

But I had hoped to spend the rest of my days with Jerry.

Soon it was time for another good-bye. Polly and Dolly hugged my neck tightly and cried. 'Good-bye, beautiful Black,' said Polly.

Harry couldn't even speak. He stroked my nose silently, then stalked out of the stable, choking back tears.

I lowered my head to little Dolly and she stroked the soft hairs near my mane. 'Daddy said to give you a kiss for him,' she said through her tears. She softly kissed my neck and then ran out as well.

I spotted Jerry being carried to the waiting carriage and I whinnied to him. I didn't want him to go. I had never been so happy since I left Birtwick Park than when I was with Jerry. He was so pale and thin. I knew the country would do him good. I only wished that I could go, too. I whinnied again at my kind master and stretched my neck towards him as far as it would go. Jerry was put into the carriage and it drove off.

I was alone again.

My Last Home

I was sold to a corn dealer, with whom Jerry thought I'd have good food and fair work. If only it had been so.

Day after day I pulled a heavy dray, loaded with bags and bags of corn. The driver was very free with his whip, laying it on whenever I slowed down at an especially steep hill. I couldn't see a way out. For two long years, I pulled his carts for him . . . until I could pull no more. One day I collapsed from sheer exhaustion. The fall seemed to take for-ever, but once I was on the ground I never wanted to get up again.

I thought I was dead.

*

I might as well have been dead. I was for sale again. It looked bleak for me . . .

This time I knew there was no kind Jerry Barker to rescue me. Now I was one of the old broken-down horses that I had looked at in pity my last time at the horse fair.

I was old and worn out. My legs were swollen. My hip bones and ribs showed sharply. My coat was ratty and dull. Only my mane and tail still had the slightest bit of my former elegance.

I took no notice of anyone who looked at me. I was beyond caring. I stood there, my head nearly touching the ground. I didn't even look up when two men passed by, commenting, 'Let's not even bother with this lot. There's nothing for them but the butcher's knife.'

The next thing I heard was a young boy's voice. 'Was that one a carriage horse, Grand-dad?' the boy asked the man standing next to him.

'He might have been anything, Willie. Look at his nostrils and ears, the shape of his neck and shoulders – there's a good deal of breeding about him. Wouldn't you say, Joe?'

'Poor old bugger,' I heard a somehow familiar voice say. I lifted my head to see who it belonged to. But the man had turned and was walking away with the two others.

'I expect we'll have better luck next month at Langley, Farmer Thoroughgood,' the familiar man said.

'It's a bigger fair,' agreed the older, ruddy-faced man.

'Much bigger,' said the man.

It was my Joe . . . but he didn't recognize me.

I looked after him, tilting my head. I couldn't lose him again. But what was I to do?

The three turned around for one last look at the horses.

'Too sad,' said the old man. 'Too sad,' he repeated. 'Not a horse here worth buying,' he said, shaking his head.

'It breaks my heart,' said Joe Green.

'Mine too,' said Farmer Thoroughgood.

They had turned their backs again, so I tried to stretch my aching neck to touch Joe with my nose. I couldn't reach.

'Shall we go, then?' asked the farmer.

Joe nodded. He followed, Willie close behind.

Watching him go, I slowly wagged my neck like I used to do in the old days when I wanted to play. I nickered feebly.

Joe hesitated for a moment. Did he hear me?

No – he kept on going.

I whinnied, but I was so weak, it was nothing like the hearty whinny of my early days.

This time Joe looked over his shoulder. He scanned the row of old horses and was about to turn away when he looked straight at me. This was my chance! I curled back my lip into a horse-smile and gathered up all my strength, wagging my head back and forth as hard as I could. I felt as if I might fall over, but I still continued.

Joe stepped forward. He looked puzzled.

I continued wagging my neck back and forth. Suddenly a look of astonishment crossed Joe's face. He walked up to me and brushed back my long black forelock to reveal the still-brilliant white star on my forehead. He gently ran his hand over it.

'Black Beauty . . .' he whispered.

I wagged my head again, this time in a mixture of joy and relief. Tears in his eyes, Joe wagged his head back at me.

I was so happy I licked Joe all over – his shoes, his trousers leg, his arm, his hand, his shoulder. I had found my old friend!

Joe threw his arms around me and hugged me tightly. Tears streamed down his face. 'I'm here, Black Beauty, I'm here. I swear I won't ever let you out of my sight again. Oh, Beauty . . . You're safe now . . .'

I huddled against him, safe at last.

I have now lived in this happy place a whole year. I spend my days on Farmer Thoroughgood's farm, grazing on the soft green grass in his meadow. My scrawny sides have filled out and my coat gleams again.

My work is easy. It's a pleasure to spend my days pulling Willie and his two giggling sisters around the farm in a light rig driven by my good friend, Joe Green. Joe is a wonderful groom, as kind as I remember.

I've been told that I'll never be sold. My strength and spirits are back. My legs aren't stiff and I can work with perfect ease. And it is wonderful to have my old name back.

But sometimes, in the early morning hours before I'm quite awake, I fancy I'm still in the orchard at Birtwick Park, watching my friends Merrylegs and Ginger chase each other around the old apple orchard. Then they pause at the top of the hill and turn towards me and perform that special little dance of long ago. I watch them spin, perfectly and elegantly, just for me. I rear giddily, just for the joy of it.

In my dreams we are young and happy, and nothing will ever separate us again.

Ever.

THE END

Some other Puffins

LITTLE WOMEN
Louisa M Alcott
Adapted by Robin Waterfield

Times are hard for the March girls

Growing up is often a difficult business. Jo, Meg, Amy and Beth have to cope with their family's lack of money and also miss their father who is away at war. They try to overcome these problems by doing new and exciting things, determined that when their father returns, they will really be 'Little Women'.

This classic story of four American girls and their adventures has been retold many times as a film and on television: this version is a faithful adaptation of the original book.

LASSIE
Sheila Black

The world's most famous dog is back!

Matt is a skateboarding heavy-metal fan, who has to come to terms with a new life in rural Virginia. Leaving his friends behind, his only companion is his faithful collie Lassie, who encourages him to explore the endless countryside and helps him make new friends.

Matt's family is threatened with another move when his father's job falls through, but he thinks of a way they can stay in the country – by running a sheep farm. After all, they do have the best grazing land around, and Lassie is an excellent sheepdog. Everyone thinks the idea will succeed . . . except their ruthless neighbour Sam Garland, who has come to believe that all the surrounding land is his.